"Those who can, do. Those
who can do more, volunteer."
- Anonymous
In honor of
Judy P.
with many thanks from the
Campbell Library

santa clara
county
library district

For Melissa
—MP

To Mateo, Tobias, and Dante
—JJ

little bee books

An imprint of Bonnier Publishing USA
251 Park Avenue South, New York, NY 10010
Text copyright © 2017 by Miranda Paul
Illustrations copyright © 2017 by Javier Joaquin
Manufactured in China LEO 0617
First Edition 10 9 8 7 6 5 4 3 2 1
Library of Congress Cataloging-in-Publication Data is
available upon request.
ISBN 978-1-4998-0480-5

littlebeebooks.com
bonnierpublishingusa.com

THE GREAT PASTA ESCAPE

written by
Miranda Paul

illustrated by
Javier Joaquin

little bee books

Since the beginning of their lives (which was earlier that morning), the pasta at the factory followed the rules.

They stuck to their own kind.

They stayed still in their packaging.

And they never spoke to humans.

Pasta that obeyed, they believed,
got sent to a super place.

So Macaroni went one way, and Rotini went another.

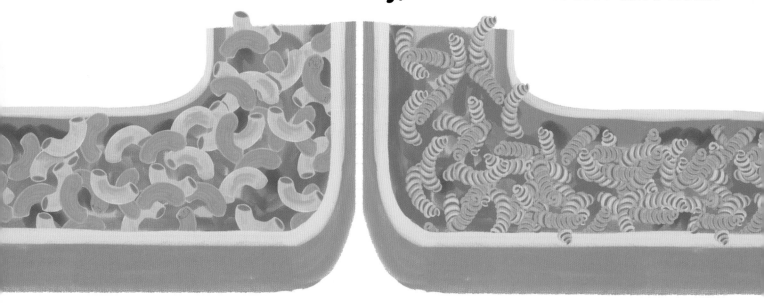

Fettuccine was boxed,

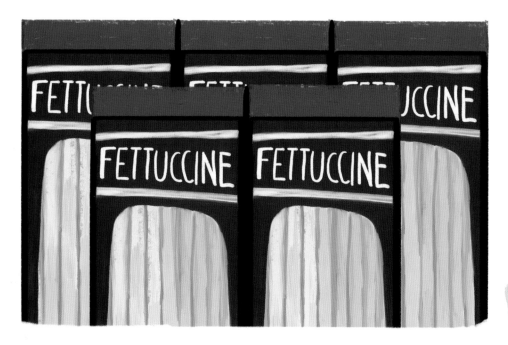

while Ramen got vacuum-sealed.

Bow Ties filled elegant canisters,

and Jumbo Shells were stuffed.

They didn't mix, move, or mingle.
They were very good noodles.

Until . . .

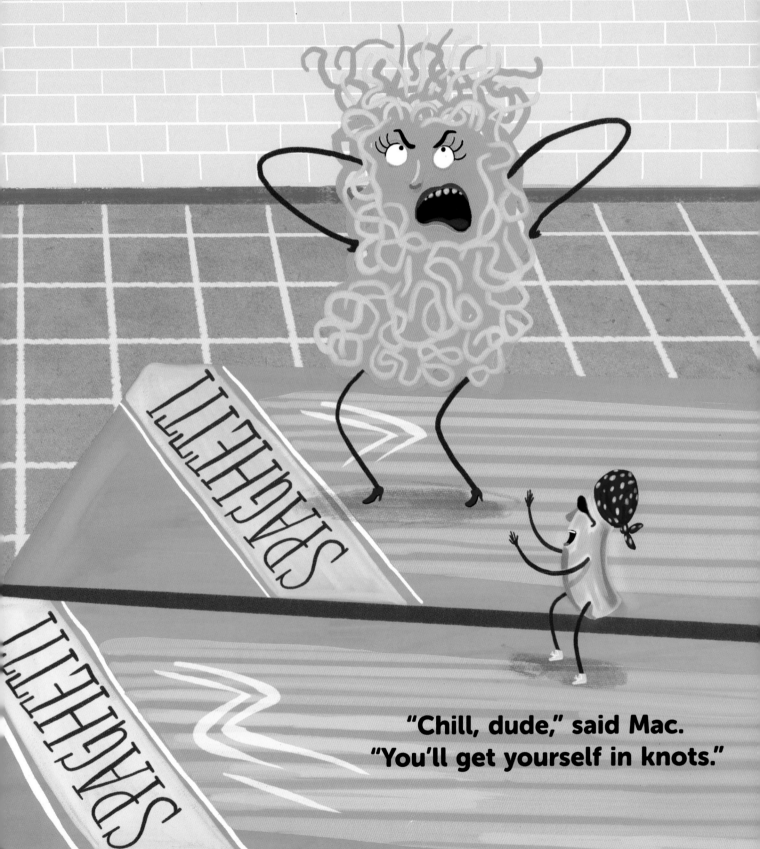

The Rotini gang chimed in.
"We present exhibits A, B, and C."

Everyone examined their packages.
The evidence was overwhelming.

Fettuccine sobbed. "Just cover me in Alfredo sauce now."

Ramen snickered. "You mean, Afraid-o sauce."

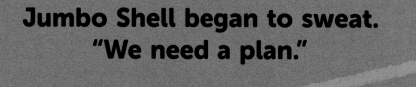

Jumbo Shell began to sweat.
"We need a plan."

"Let's hide," said
Fettuccine.

"Now let's not get carried away. . . ." said Mac. "And what about that super place we've been hearing and dreaming about?"

"Forget Spaghetti," said a Rotini. **"If we execute this plan perfectly, it will work. . . . But it means sacrificing the Ravioli. It's the only way."**

The Ravioli were outraged.
They called the Tortellini for backup.

"Fiiiiiight!" yelled Ramen.
Chaos broke out on the floor.

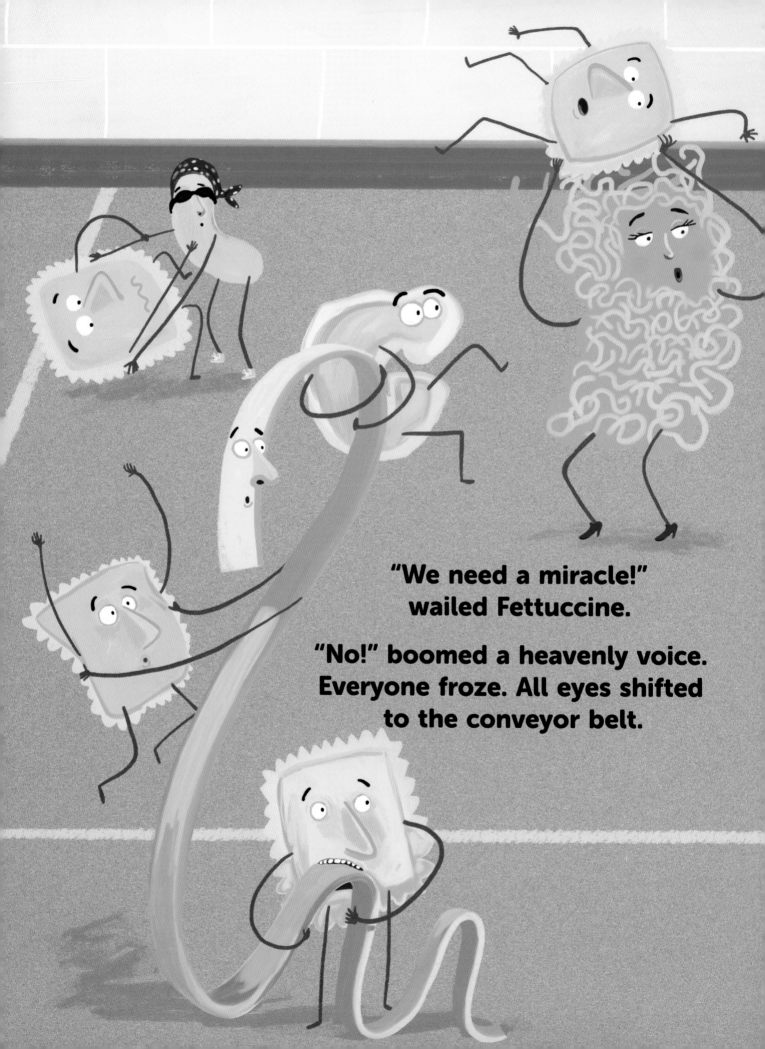

"We need a miracle!" wailed Fettuccine.

"No!" boomed a heavenly voice. Everyone froze. All eyes shifted to the conveyor belt.

"You need . . . an angel."

"It's simple," said Angel Hair.
"We just have to use our noodles. Together."

She huddled them all and they quickly cooked up the perfect plan.

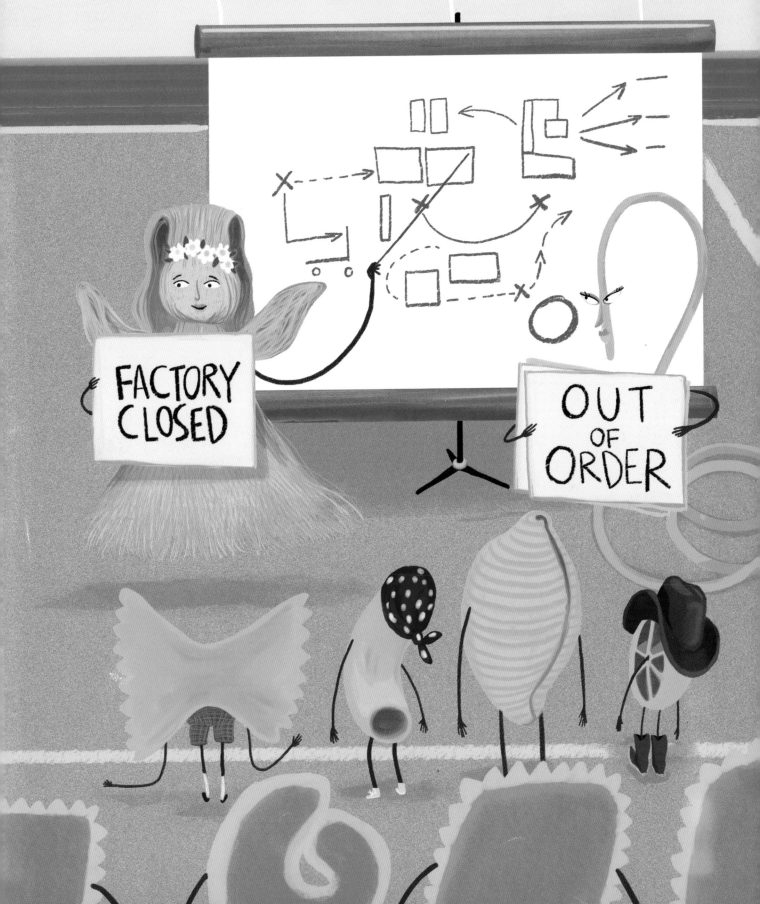

MENU

GUIDE TO PASTA SHAPES!

Angel Hair

Macaroni

Shell

Bow Tie (Farfalle)

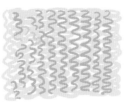

Ramen

Spaghetti

Fettuccine

Ravioli

Tortellini

Lasagne

Rigatoni

Wagon Wheel (Rotelle)

Linguine

Rotini

Ziti